LITTLE MISS DOTTY
has a dotty day out

Original concept by Roger Hargreaves
Illustrated and written by Adam Hargreaves

MR. MEN   LITTLE MISS

MR MEN and LITTLE MISS™ & © 1998 Mrs Roger Hargreaves.
World International

Little Miss Dotty is every bit as dotty as her name suggests.

For instance, last year, Miss Dotty carpeted her garden path!

She lives in Nonsenseland, where the grass is blue and the trees are red, a place which is every bit as dotty as Miss Dotty.

In Nonsenseland all the pigs have televisions ...

... and wear slippers.

One day, while she was walking through Whoopee Wood, she met her two friends, Mr Silly and Mr Nonsense.

"Hello," said Miss Dotty.

"Hello," said Mr Silly and Mr Nonsense at the same time.

Mr Silly was carrying a saw.

"We're going to make a see-saw," said Mr Nonsense. "Would you like to join in?"

"Yes please," said Miss Dotty, who had been wondering what to do.

So the three of them set off.

They walked and they walked and they walked a long, long way until they came to the seaside.

But being Nonsenseland the sand wasn't yellow, it was pink.

When they got to the water's edge Mr Silly threw the saw in!

Have you ever heard of anything so silly?

"Brilliant," said Mr Nonsense.

"That's the best sea-saw ever," agreed Miss Dotty.

"What shall we do now?" said Mr Silly.

"Let's go for a paddle," suggested Miss Dotty.

So they went to the shop on the pier and each bought a paddle!

"That was fun," said Mr Nonsense. "What next?"

"Let's dig in the sand," said Mr Silly.

"Good idea," said Miss Dotty.

So they went down to the beach and dug a big hole ...

... and then filled it in!

"I did enjoy that," grinned Mr Nonsense.

"I'm hungry," said Miss Dotty. "What shall we eat?"

"Easy peasy," said Mr Nonsense, "Sandwiches!"

And I'm sure you can guess what they did next.

That's right!

They put sand between slices of buttered bread and ate sand sandwiches!

Can you imagine anything more dotty!

After lunch they drew in the sand ...

with crayons!

And they sunbathed ...

under umbrellas!

The sun was setting as they walked all the long way back to Miss Dotty's house and had supper together.

"We must do that again," said Miss Dotty.

"We must," agreed the other two.

And they got up from the table and went back to the beach!

"It's dark, isn't it?" said Miss Dotty.

RETURN THIS WHOLE PAGE

Join Our Club!

MR. MEN & Little Miss CLUB

When you become a member of the fantastic Mr Men and Little Miss Club you'll receive a personal letter from Mr Happy and Little Miss Giggles, a club badge with your name, and a superb Welcome Pack (pictured below right).

You'll also get birthday and Christmas cards from the Mr Men and Little Misses, 2 newsletters crammed with special offers, privileges and news, and a copy of the 12 page Mr Men catalogue which includes great party ideas.

If it were on sale in the shops, the Welcome Pack alone might cost around £13. But a year's membership is just £9.99 (plus 73p postage) with a 14 day money-back guarantee if you are not delighted!

HOW TO APPLY To apply for any of these three great offers, ask an adult to complete the coupon below and send it with appropriate payment and tokens (where required) to: Mr Men Offers, PO Box 7, Manchester M19 2HD. Credit card orders for Club membership ONLY by telephone, please call: 01403 242727.

To be completed by an adult

❏ **1.** Please send a poster and door hanger as selected overleaf. I enclose six tokens and a 50p coin for post (coin not required if you are also taking up 2. or 3. below).

❏ **2.** Please send ___ Mr Men Library case(s) and ___ Little Miss Library case(s) at £5.49 each.

❏ **3.** Please enrol the following in the Mr Men & Little Miss Club at £10.72 (inc postage)

Fan's Name:_____Fan's Address:_____

_____Post Code:_____Date of birth:___/___/___

Your Name:_____Your Address:_____

Post Code:_____Name of parent or guardian (if not you):_____

Total amount due: £_____ (£5.49 per Library Case, £10.72 per Club membership)

❏ I enclose a cheque or postal order payable to Egmont World Limited.

❏ Please charge my MasterCard / Visa account.

Card number: | | | | | | | | | | | | | | | | |

Expiry Date: ____/____   Signature: _____

Data Protection Act: If you do **not** wish to receive other family offers from us or companies we recommend, please tick this box ❏. Offer applies to UK only

3 Great Offers For Mr Men Fans

1 FREE Door Hangers and Posters

In every Mr Men and Little Miss Book like this one you will find a special token. Collect 6 and we will send you either a brilliant Mr. Men or Little Miss poster and a Mr Men or Little Miss double sided, full colour, bedroom door hanger. Apply using the coupon overleaf, enclosing six tokens and a 50p coin for your choice of two items.

Egmont World tokens can be used towards any other Egmont World / World International token scheme promotions., in early learning and story / activity books.

Posters: Tick your preferred choice of either Mr Men ☐ or Little Miss ☐

Door Hangers: Choose from: Mr. Nosey & Mr Muddle ☐, Mr Greedy & Mr Lazy ☐, Mr Tickle & Mr Grumpy ☐, Mr Slow & Mr Busy ☐ Mr Messy & Mr Quiet ☐, Mr Perfect & Mr Forgetful ☐, Little Miss Fun & Little Miss Late ☐, Little Miss Helpful & Little Miss Tidy ☐, Little Miss Busy & Little Miss Brainy ☐, Little Miss Star & Little Miss Fun ☐. (Please tick)

2 Mr Men Library Boxes

Keep your growing collection of Mr Men and Little Miss books in these superb library boxes. With an integral carrying handle and stay-closed fastener, these full colour, plastic boxes are fantastic. They are just £5.49 each including postage. Order overleaf.

3 Join The Club

To join the fantastic Mr Men & Little Miss Club, check out the page overleaf NOW!

Allow 28 days for delivery. We reserve the right to change the terms of this offer at any time but we offer a 14 day money back guarantee. The money-back guarantee does not affect your statutory rights. Birthday and Christmas cards are sent care of parent/guardians in advance of the day. After 31/12/00 please call to check that the offer details are still correct.

MR MEN and LITTLE MISS™ & © 1998 Mrs. Roger Hargreaves